KINKY CRAVINGS

Erotic Scenes Around The House

Jamal Walker

I'd like to dedicate this book to those of you who find themselves locked up inside. By this I mean you are either yet to find yourself or you know what you like sexually however you are too afraid to speak on it openly.

This book will open your eyes and educate you that you are not the only one to have these kinky cravings and that these are usual.

For those of you already doing everything you like maybe theres something in here you are yet to try. Good Luck!

I love you all and appreciate your support.

CONTENTS

KINKY CRAVINGS

THE BEDROOM

I didn't own the house.

But I walked as I did.

My pace was calm and calculated, each step effusing a certain dominance that would make perfect sense if I were stepping into my bedroom. I didn't consider my footsteps noisy, but when Melissa looked away from her phone screen, there was no mistaking the sound of my footsteps had made it to her ears.

She sat unmoving, her back glued to the backrest of her pink-sheeted king-sized bed. Once our eyes connected, my chest heaved and my breath turned noticeably heavier, evidence of my blood heating in my veins, the same way it always did whenever my body ached for the slender yet curvaceous body of my Caucasian lover. Before her, I had wrongly believed that a slender woman had no capacity for a massive endowment. But everything changed when I met her.

It didn't matter that Melissa Osborne and I had been dating for three years already; I was yet to come to terms with the science behind her endowment. Try as I might, I could never understand how a woman as delicately thin as her could keep her spine straight as a ruler even though the double D darlings on her chest accounted for a noteworthy percentage of her weight.

"I thought you wanted some time alone." She looked away from me and returned her attention to her phone. "I didn't want to disturb."

Although she was no longer looking in my direction, I could tell that a crossed look had crept into those baby blue eyes. Her voice had dropped just before she looked away from me. That was all I needed to know that she hated every moment I'd chosen the EPL over her. It was barely even twenty minutes into the first half of the game and a nagging feeling in my heart had me retracing my steps. It had brought me back to her.

I closed the door behind me and took another step further into the room. "Fuck the match. I can always watch a replay."

She looked up at me, and this time, I caught a gleam in her eyes. Besides it though, there was an apparent confusion that caused her full brows to wrinkle. It told me there was an unvoiced question on her mind.

"Why so quiet?" I asked with a crooked smile.

She smiled back at me, "Trying to understand why you would ditch your almighty soccer."

She rolled her eyes at me and lowered her eyes once again. I had given up on watching the match just so I could spend time with her. And she was about to give her phone all of her attention?

Not on my watch!

"Same reason why you are also gonna put away that phone, babe." Halting beside the bed, I locked the fingers of my right hand around the top of her phone and slowly slid the device out of her hand.

She probably hadn't seen this coming, but there was no resistance. Her only reaction was a backward tilt of her head so she could look up into my eyes. Styled in a messy pony, her wavy blonde hair dipped toward her ass as she looked up at me. From the way her hair swayed behind her, it was tickling her lower back which was left uncovered by the white crop top she paired with her green cargo joggers.

Without another word, I set down her phone on the nightstand beside me. Melissa's eyes were on me the whole time, watching with a certain droop that could make me swear she had some sliminess already building up between her thighs. I placed my right hand on the left side of her face, worked my way down to her narrow chin and cupped her face with both hands. Her parting lips told her how badly she anticipated a kiss. I could feel her heartbeat slowing as she awaited the brush of my lips on hers.

I stared deeply into her eyes and then I leaned in toward her. Her lips called out to me,

It was a call I would gladly answer.

But first…

I reached for her right ear instead. "I think it's time for bed."

I let go of her and moved to straighten my spine, but she reached for me at once.

"No!" Her voice was a growl.

She grabbed me by the lapel of my short-sleeved black top and yanked me down toward her. My face was just above hers, barely even an inch away. I could feel her breath on my face, tickling my African American skin as well as the generous spray of stubbles that had become a part of my identity since I turned twenty-seven. Hell, I could even hear her breath, rough and raspy, making a graceless entry into my ears.

"You're just gonna make me want you and leave me in this state?" She sucked in a noisy breath and nibbled at her lower lip.

"What state exactly?" I feigned innocence to her 'state'.

Her teeth released her lower lip, and just as I expected, she left my question hanging, just so she wouldn't say the dirty words on her mind. Her innocence, it seemed, was a part of her that was bent on surviving into her twenties. And I was a man bent on making this innocence a sweet memory.

"I think it's time for bed." My voice was louder than it had been the first time I said these words, as though she hadn't heard me the first time.

Her only response was a subtle nod.

Or so I thought until I heard her speak.

"Okay," she said.

"Well...unless..." I leaned toward her, and this time, I let my lips brush hers.

She held her breath. "Unless what?"

"Well, unless you have other plans, baby girl, and..." I moved forward. "And from all indications, it seems like you do."

"I want you," she whispered.

I smiled at her. "Say it again."

My voice was a whisper, just like hers.

"I want—" she started.

But I didn't give her a chance to finish. I leaned into her and placed my lips against hers. She let out a gasp, her hands reaching for my arms and pulling me even closer. My eyelids fell over my eyes, shutting out the world and everything in it so all I could see was a sea of lustrous black. While I stared off into space, I kissed her harder, deeper, each move of my lips shoving her toward breathlessness.

My breath turned erratic, causing my chest to rise and fall rhythmically.

She moaned against my lips and I opened my eyes just in time to see her eyes rolling back in their sockets. Her eyelids moved slowly to conceal her pupils. I wrapped my lips around her bottom lip. Her lip was soft and moist, begging for a bite, so I slowly let my teeth sink into the soft flesh. I sucked on her lip and slowly unbalanced myself, deepening the kiss with an intensity that led her backward until her body was flat against the mattress.

I slowly mounted her, pinning her to the bed with my right knee between her legs. Her eyes were open now, staring deep into my soul as I smothered her neck with lingering kisses. The look in my eyes was just as intense, if not even more intense. I broke the kiss for a moment, just so I could feast my eye on even the subtle details on her face.

"You're so beautiful," I said.

Her cheeks heated up, as expected. When she blushed like that, I knew better than to expect a word from her. Maybe this time would be different and she would say a word, but I didn't wait to find out. I wrapped my left arm around her neck and pulled her in for yet another kiss. While my kiss overpowered her into breathlessness, I nibbled at her lower lip and forced her head deeper into the springs of the bed. With an almost animalistic growl, I leaned back, grabbed the hem of her top and pulled the obtrusive fabric over her head.

I leaned away from her and took a moment to worship her nude presence, staring hard enough to take a mental photo of her. My eyes roaming her full-frontal nudity, I slowly set down her crop top and caressed her perky breasts with my sultry gaze. Her nipples were hard, begging to be groped already. They had been pressing into the fabric of her crop top, and now, without the fabric in the way, they revelled in the calm breeze permeating the room.

Goosebumps erupted all over her skin, interrupting the flawless smoothness she was known for. I placed my hands on her back and glided my long fingers against her spine. My pace was slow and steady as my fingers followed the prominent line until they disappeared beneath her joggers. She gasped and held on to me, and after I had trailed the length of her ass crack for a few heart-pacing moments, I settled her on her back and slowly mounted her until my full weight settled on her slender body, crushing her into the bed. I glued myself to her. Chest to chest; lips to lips; tongues interlocked.

My hands trailed down her body and once they brushed the waistband of her joggers, I yanked down the fabric, forcing it under her ass. In a motion as fluid as air, I continued to drag down the fabric, and while I was at it, I kept my lips locked around hers.

I wanted to grab every inch of Melissa's body, to touch her everywhere at once and feel her heat beneath my finger pads. Once her joggers set was out of the way, I flung off the fabric without caring to see where it landed. My hands roamed her body, from her nipples to her neck and her back to her ass until they slid between her legs and cupped her pussy. She moaned against my lips, her voice just as soft as her breath.

I led my lips away from hers and peppered kisses down her body, only stopping briefly to suck both nipples before proceeding past her inverted belly button and toward her pussy. I had not forgotten her white pantie when I rid her of her underwear. And now, after kissing her pussy through the thin fabric, I yanked down the article of clothing and tossed it in the same direction I had tossed her joggers.

"We should shower now," I said.

"But—" she protested.

I shut her up with a much-needed correction of the words I had just said. "Must."

There now. All fixed.

We must shower now. Those words were an order she couldn't dare defy.

THE BATHROOM

I wanted Melissa in front of me while we headed for the bath-room, just so I could watch her ass wiggle with each step she took. Her steps were gracious and calculated, and her hips swayed with the elegance of a queen. Her scent was not overpowering enough to dull out the scent of the air freshener wafting around the house, yet it was the only scent pleasing to my senses. I ached to be closer to her and flood my lungs with more of her scent until it was the only thing slipping through my nostrils.

She stepped into the bathroom and I behind her, following each step. I crept up behind her and wrapped my arms around her body. My dark skin contrasted starkly with her olive skin, yet it felt just right, in the same way, the beautiful blue of her eyes felt just right even though it starkly contrasted with the pale yellow of her hair. She leaned into me in a wordless plea for a caress. My left hand rose to her face and caressed her sweat-coated right cheek while I softly pressed my face into hers, cheek to cheek. Body to body, we shuffled across the bathroom floor. My pelvis moulded into hers, and my pectorals connected with her chest. She wiggled in my arms, as though teasing my sculptured pectoral muscles with her breasts.

Entwined my passion, we became one in complete sync. I kissed her again, gently stroking her neck and dragging my fingers to her lower back while simultaneously leading her to the shower. With my free hand, I turned on the shower and led her into the shower compartment. She shuddered and clung to me as the first drops of water made it to her skin. Steam rose around us, latched on to the cold glass of the compartment and obstructed my view of the other side of the glass.

I liked it that way. With Melissa, I needed no distractions. Her beauty had me pledging my undivided attention to her. I stepped back to admire her beauty, my eyes following the drops of water travelling down her cleavage and all the way down to her engorged clit. I settled on the bench on the left side of the shower and watched her detach the showerhead from the mount. Her eyes were locked on mine, hardening my cock even without her touch. She slowly lowered herself to a seating position and prepared herself with crossed legs. Decreasing the height of the jets as they began to aim at her clit, she exhaled briskly in anticipation of the pleasure that would soon follow.

Angling the jets of the showerhead more precisely, she further parted the slits in her labia with jets of warm water. My heart paced excitedly as I watched her teasing her clit. The sensual sight brought a range of powerful sensations to me, triggering a surge of hormones all over my body.

To spice things up, I decided to flush a burst of water through the head onto her throbbing clit. Her boy released delicate pheromones into the steamy air as the cold sensation raced through her body with excitement, allowing for her first minor orgasm.

My brain received a shot of her steamy hot love, spurring me to sit behind her with my legs on both sides of her and her body leaning into mine. I snaked my arms around her body and cupped her left breast with my left hand. My right hand proceeded down her body, making its way beyond her bikini line while I simultaneously massaged the warm water into her left breast to soften the muscles behind her large dark areola until she shuddered in my arms with her head on my shoulder. Using my ring and index finger to part her, my middle finger created a narrow path for itself. On my way back up, I glided freely towards her clit, rousing her with the thought of stimulating the sensitive bud. She gasped in anticipation, but I made a U-turn and a disappointed sigh escaped her lips.

"Please..." she cried.

"Or what?" I asked, even though I knew what her response would be.

"Or I'll do it myself." She brought her right hand to her clit but I was quick to stop her from interrupting my slow stimulation of her clit.

"Self-control." I kissed her left ear lobe and nibbled at it. "Learn it."

With her lips held apart, I gently pushed back the soft smooth textures of skin enclosing the mini plum-like feature to her pussy. I savoured the wet and silky texture of her pussy and rotated my middle finger on her hypersensitive clit.

"Oh God!" she moaned, grasping me tightly. "Oh, God! Please don't stop!"

Her voice was between a moan and a cry, her words interrupted by raspy breaths. A twitch of her muscles told me she was just about to change position—an act that would defeat my plans of having full control over her body. I placed my legs over her knees to stop her from being able to change position. Once I gained full control over her body, I had her right where I wanted her.

"A safe word..." I said.

A safe word was her only way out of my grip.

"What?" she asked.

"Do you have one?" I stimulated her clit with my fingers as I spoke.

Her only response was a lazy moan. Once the sound made it to my ears, I knew better than to expect a safe word. Melissa was enjoying this too much to want a way out. My fingers kept rotating between her legs, teasing her until each digit was drenched with her stick fluid. Her legs trembled noticeably and she fought to close them, but I forced them to stay open as I worked her with my now slippery fingers. I held her in place, letting wave after wave of orgasm pass over her.

She pushed back against me, her back flattening against my chest. "Jackpot!"

"Oh yeah?"

"My safe word," she explained. "Oh, God..."

She pushed against me again, as though she were trying to break free from my hold, and although she desperately needed a breather, I kept on working her with my fingers, She flung her head back and settled it on my left shoulder. In response, I quickened the rotation of my finger. I added a second finger and shoved her to yet another climax. She tensed up around my fingers and ejected her juices all over my fingers. The sensation of the clear liquid escaping her throbbing hole kept her at the peak of her orgasm, forcing her to break free from my grasp and begin rubbing away at the sensation.

I withdrew my fingers just enough to let her rub away the ache between her legs. A deep exhalation marked the end of her orgasm, and she looked up into my eyes with a satisfied sigh fleeing her parted lips. All smiled, I patted the crux of her legs. She clenched up almost instantly, and then she turned around on all fours. When she stared at me with those beautiful amorous eyes, with her huge breasts hanging down her chest, it was impossible not to touch her all over again.

This time though, I let her lead. She crawled forward and planted a soft kiss on my lips. Her fingers brushed my cock, eliciting a moan from my lips.

I broke the kiss and stared deeply into her eyes. "We should shower now."

She nodded vigorously.

I helped her to her feet and after helping each other with a quick wash, we stepped out of the shower compartment. I grabbed a white towel and began to dry her from top to bottom. Working my way down, I finished in a kneeling position and planted a kiss on her soft belly. Her stomach clenched with a sharp inhalation. I worked my way around her bikini line.

I looked up into her eyes for a go-ahead. Her chest heaving with another deep breath, she smiled sheepishly and turned away from me. When she advanced toward the wooden-framed oval mirror covering up a few inches of the wall, I knew she wanted me to follow. I rose to my feet, hanged the now damp towel and headed for her sexy body. Her body was starting to get wet again, no thanks to the drops of water escaping her hair. My eyes followed the streaks of water as they created a damp path to her ass and soon got lost in her ass crack.

She opened the first drawer of the marble top cabinet beneath the mirror and produced a red set of matching lace underwear I got her for her twenty-first birthday. I stared admiringly at her reflection in the mirror as she concealed her most feminine parts beneath the delicate fabric of her underwear. I placed my hands on her waist and she welcomed my touch with a deep smile.

I pulled her back toward my body and worked my head around her damp hair to find her neck. My eyes were trained on the mirror the whole time, staring deep into the reflection of her eyes. Upon finding her neck, I peppered kisses across her delicate skin until every inch was covered with my essence. I slowly turned her around to face me and a knowing smile crossed her lips.

She could already guess what I was about to do, yet a small gasp slipped past her lips when I swept her off the floor and settled her on the warm marble surface of the cabinet. My eyes trailed her torso until they settled on the point where her pussy lips kissed the marble. I didn't need to look up at the mirror to know that a gleam crept into my eyes as I marvelled at the thickness of her pussy pushing through the purpose cut hole in the lace material.

I stepped in toward her, claimed my place between her legs and wrapped my arms around her. My lips found hers in a soft kiss which soon turned demanding as I craved more of her on my taste buds. She moaned into my mouth and a similar sound escaped my lips. Our tongues lashed out as we searched for acceptance within one another. My hands raced behind her to undo the clasp of her bra. Barely a moment had passed since we detached our bodies from each other, yet I was already aching for yet another moment of skin to skin connection—a moment in which our souls would connect on a fibre optic level of latency, causing an eruption of sensory emotions to rush to our brains.

When I had watched Melissa clad herself in her underwear, the thought of dressing up had not crossed my mind. Even while I watched her slide the lace onto her skin, I had known that dressing up was a total waste. I was not about to retire from touching her so quickly. Not when there remained some territories left unexplored. I pulled her forward so the weight of her body settled on me and not her ass. Her ass detached from the marble and I slid my hands beneath her to grab her ass cheeks.

But Melissa had a plan of her own. Or so it seemed when she leaned back on the marble and parted her legs some more. I withdrew my hands from her ass and settled them on her upper thighs. She brought her between her thighs and slowly parted her pearly gates, granting me entrance into her wet snatch. I planted my stiff cock at her opening and pushed through her sphincter with my girth. We wrapped our arms around each other in confirmation of mutual love and acceptance. I thrust harder, reaching deep enough to elicit a raspy gasp from her.

Deep moans proceeded through my lips as I started to thrust in a slow steady rhythm. Her juices coated every inch of my hard cock, helping me to slide through at a smoother rate. I could feel my blood pumping through me, and could hear the loudness of her pounding heart. My cock started to pulse. Each pulsation earned a counteracting contraction of her soft warm pussy, and subsequently smooth friction as I kept pumping her.

Our breaths synchronized, our hearts thumping as one as we reached new heights of ecstasy. She gripped me tighter, urging me to go deeper until she roared with her orgasm. Barely a moment after she came, I shot a thick glob of cum inside of her.

Still shaken from the wave of pleasure, we held on to each other until our pacing hearts neared normalcy. I slowly pulled out of her, and our creamy mix sought an escape from her gaping hole. Gripping her thighs to hold her steady, I bent down to lick her juices back inside of her, where they belonged.

THE HALLWAY

When Melissa and I walked down the hallway, we maintained our usual position. She led the way, her glorious figure hardening up my cock with each graceful sway of her hips. I was starting to crave her warm embrace all over again. I doubled my pace and grabbed her left arm, which I yanked hard toward my body, pulling her back into a twirl. I stared into her face, my eyes trained at her soft tender lips as she returned my gaze.

We stood there in the hallway, our bodies as immobile as the walls around us. After a moment, I loosened my grip on her and lowered myself onto my right knee while my eyes stayed fixated on hers. Her lotus flower stared directly into my face, forcing me to notice its greatness. I kissed my left index finger and my thumb and placed my finger pads on her sphincter. Adding a gentle pressure, I eased my fingers forward, toward the warmth of her slippery walls. And then, without a word, I pulled my hand away. My heart was starting to beat twice as fast, supplying blood to my already engorging cock. Melissa placed her soft hands on my firm shoulders—a wordless plea for me to take her already.

I gently shoved her backwards, into the cold wall. The bold gesture detached her from reality and she shuddered against the wall. I stuck out my tongue and parted her meaty pussy lips with it. The spit-coated tip of my tongue dipped inside of her, tasting the entrance of her honeycomb and depositing her delicious juices on my taste buds. I added a slight pressure to my tongue, parting her even further. I cupped her bouncy butt with my hands. My grip on her ass tightened as my face fell deep into her rivers.

It took a moment, however, for me to realize just how incorrect my grip was. Parting her legs, I grabbed her ass and settled her thighs on my forearm. This position allowed me to dig deeper, devouring her with my tongue. I felt her hand behind my head, applying pressure to her forbidden fruit. She gasped and whimpered as I touched new areas her fingers had previously missed or brushed over. I followed her rhythm, riding in sync toward orgasm. I gripped her ass harder as I felt the pressure of her pumping blood expanding her feminine folds. I let out a heavy breath as we reached the towers of her climax, and then I accelerated the rhythm of my tongue's connections to her clit.

Supporting herself with her back against the wall, Melissa rode my face with aggression I hadn't seen coming. Fighting not to bite her, I followed her stride, pleasing her with my tongue until another wave of orgasm left her shaken. Her breath was hard and fast, erupting in irregular bursts. Mine was no different. Desperate for a breather, I detached my tongue from her, and while I flooded my lungs with oxygen, I simultaneously slid my index finger into her honeycomb. Hitting her G-spot, I sent her into a ripple of fiery shivers causing her honey to gush out of her. I caught her sweetness in my mouth and stood to face her.

Her eyes were squeezed shut, blocking out every sight. And in her oblivion, I leaned forward for a kiss, sharing with her the juiciness I had just picked up from her raw pussy. Once every trace of her sweet nectar was gone, I pulled back to stare at her glossy lips. She was yet to recover from the maddening sensations her orgasm had left in its wake. So, I held her tightly, helping her remain on her feet as she tried to quell the tremor in her chest.

THE WALK-IN WARDROBE

Wearing nothing but our textured skin, Melissa and I stepped into her ensuite open plan wardrobe. She hurried to the mirror, as though her life depended on her keeping track of even the most recent developments on her face and body. I grabbed a bottle of massage oil from a shelf and stood behind her. From the eagerness with which her eyes roamed her body, I could tell she was checking out all the little things she categorized as her imperfections.

"You're beautiful, baby," I said, pouring the massage oil on her back and watching it drip to her ass. "I see no flaws. Just a beautiful sexy woman who completes me."

She lowered her head, accepting both my words and the soothing effect of the warm oil on her skin. "You're so sweet."

"Only for you babe." I set down the bottle and fixated my eyes on the drops of oil gliding toward her ass.

Each run of oil took a unique path as they glided through and around the fine sensory hairs of her body. Once the oil reached her ass crack, I bent her over, creating an open entrance for it to continue. I placed my hands on her glistening ass and started to knead her soft oily skin in a circular motion. Her ass cheeks parted and rejoined gracefully, and as her body soaked up the oil, her complexion deepened, becoming more vibrant in response to my touch. I positioned myself behind her ass cheeks and vertically filled her ass crack with my cock. I glided my hand from the bottom to the top of her back, then around to her front, cupping her boobs until the meaty pair glistened with oil.

Upon establishing a firm grip, I pulled her placed her head on my left shoulder and stared into the mirror to admire her beautiful reflection. I picked up the bottle of oil again, and drizzled some oil on the front of her body, purposefully covering her nipples. I watched as she became more and more relaxed against my body, enticing me to begin smothering the liquid into her chest and tummy. She gripped my quadriceps as I continue to knead her breast, feeling every texture as my hands glided against her flawless skin.

Moving down towards her tummy, I set my destination for the gap in between her legs. A knowing smile graced her lips, and her eyes shut right after, allowing no distractions as she received every sensory stimulation I would soon offer. As I approached my destination, my middle and ring finger parted to modify the natural position of her inner labia, thus creating a perfect fit when my knuckles brushed her clit. The forearm of my other arm kept her breasts company as I placed them directly beneath the impressive rack like a bra holding them up while holding our bodies firmly together.

Subduing her in this position allowed me to take full control of her temple. I begin to glissade around her clitoral hood, causing a smooth run of warm liquid to proceed out of her pulsating hole. Welcoming this juiciness, I took a tour around her labia, spreading the moisture and heightening her clitoral sense. The slow unhurried beats of her heart informed me that she was nearing her orgasm. I could feel my blood pumping into my vessel like a car jack as it rose with every pump. The ascendance led to a cold sensation at the point of contact with the bottom of her ass cheeks. The shock sent a firm grip to my hand playing with her labia. My middle and ring finger enter her in a curved motion, encouraging me to press my penis against her checks trying to cut through the cheeks like a knife. With a tight grip on my legs, she raised herself in an apparent effort to relieve the pressure from within.

"God, Melissa!" I growled into her left ear. "I can't take this any-more..."

"Then don't..." she urged, her voice just as raspy as mine. "Please —"

A startled gasp cut her off as I pushed her against the mirror. She threw her hands out onto the mirror as though I was about to frisk her. Her arching back caused her ass to shoot out toward me. I spanked her left ass cheek and she looked back at me with a naughty smile.

"You love it when I hit you like this, don't you, you dirty little girl?" I rubbed the sore spot I had just spanked.

"Oh yes, daddy!"

I spanked her right ass cheek. She winced and gasped, but didn't dare move away from me or break her gaze.

"Oh!" Another wince as I spanked her again, harder this time.

She nibbled at her lower lip to keep from crying.

I spread her ass cheeks and looked down for her opening. She returned her attention to the mirror and grabbed my endowment, which I hastily slipped through her tightness. An eruption of heat shot through the head of my cock as we connected skin to skin. I steadied myself, placing my hands on both sides of her ass as I began to thrust, gently breaking every resistance as I pushed deeper and deeper.

She sucked in a deep breath. "Oh yes! Harder, daddy! Fuck my tight ass, please..."

She bowed her head and cried out as I tore through her, settling my cock balls-deep inside her tight ass. I moved my pelvis faster, causing her breasts to swing back and forth on her chest. My heartbeat accelerated as I kept thrusting, and from her shallow breaths, I knew hers was no different.

I detached one hand from her bottom and took a path under her arms to wrap my hand around her throat. Once clinched, I picked up the pace, fucking her harder than I thought she could bear. Muscles throbbed dangerously on her neck and a scream tore her lips apart as my cock pushed hard against her walls. Once I added some more pressure, she reversed the arch in her back, causing my cock to pop out of her. If she had a safe word, then this would have been the moment to use it.

I whirled her around and guided her to her knees. My cock slipped between her lips and she parted those lips even further to accommodate my girth. Quickly grabbing my cock hand, she worked it with a series of twist and jerk movements. My breathing heightened, and as I neared my orgasm, she aimed my cock at the ceiling and began to suck on my balls.

With a groan, I gripped the top of the cabinet to steady myself as I exploded with a shuddering orgasm. My cock pulsed with ecstasy and she wrapped her lips around my shaft at once, directing my thick creamy load into her throat.

Weak at my knees, I dropped to the floor. I crept toward her and fingered her juicy pussy with an urgency that had her gripping my shoulders for support. I only pulled away when a short spray of cum leaked over my fingers.

THE STAIRCASE

Fully clothed, Melissa and I exited the walk-in wardrobe wearing. She was clad in a one fitted latex black suit that outlined every sexy curve and contour of her body. She, however, would not get to stand on her feet anytime soon; not when she was on the leash, on all fours and at my feet. Propelling her forward with the leash, I led her on all fours toward the stairway leading to the top floor of her apartment. She looked up at me and licked her lips, making them glisten all over again.

She seemed to have forgotten that my fingers of my right hand were wrapped around a leather whip. I tightened my hold on the device and whipped her hard across her left ass, sending tenacious vibrations to her nerve endings. We arrived at the top of the cold metal spiral staircase and I wrapped the leash tighter around my fist, reducing the available slack. She positioned herself on her knees where she quietly awaited my next command.

Standing in front of her, I stared deeply into her eyes and I moved my whip up her body. Once the whip reached her neck, she lifted her head higher with apparent anxiety. I placed a firm hand on her face and stroked her lips with my thumb. My thumb halted between her lips and poked its way into her mouth. She parted her lips for a smooth entrance and I bent forward to replace my thumb with my lips.

After a brief kiss, I straightened my spine and pulled her leash, forcing her head closer to the zipper of my pants. With a quick response to maintain her balance, she grabbed my thighs to steady herself. Once her balance was restored, she stared deeply into my eyes and began to unbutton my jeans. As she disengaged my zip, my bulge of love becomes more apparent, forcing its way through my boxers. She yanked down my pants and released my thick yet flaccid cock. Leaning to one side, it stared into her face requesting for a breath of life.

With a smile, she cupped my sack and flicked her tongue around the fat head of my cock, bathing me in enough spit to make for a smooth penetration. She slipped her head down until she was gagging on my cock. She sucked hard, her head bobbing along my shaft and smearing every inch with spit while her hands kneaded my balls, sending multiple sensational ripples through me.

She moved away from my cock and began to suck on my balls instead. Her fingers wrapped around my cock, stroking my full length as she kept sucking my balls. I grabbed the cold metal railing of the staircase and raised my right leg for a more intimate connection. With one foot now on the bannister, I pushed your head further backwards, leading her to my dark hole. You moved in cautiously, taking your first lick, of questioned acceptance. With an excepted discretion, she grabbed me as I turned around and bent over, pushing my ass into her pretty face with the tension of the leash giving her no way out.

She parted my ass cheeks and forced her tongue deep into me, I groaned deeply, my rear muscles relaxing as I surrendered to the pleasure. I glanced down and found a clear liquid escaping your crotchless latex suit. At this moment I knew she was ready for something more intense. Stretching my whip between my legs, I prepared to make the connection. With no prior warning, I struck, startling her clit with an unforeseen sensation.

"Ouch!" She popped my cock out of her mouth and tried to retreat.

Not a chance. I spun around, pulled her halfway down the stairs and positioned her for doggy-style.

"Round, smooth and juicy..." I smacked her ass, causing a ripple effect similar to the motion of water.

Engaging my two hands, I spread her ass cheeks to create a path for my endowment. Her succulent lips were slick with her juices. They parted in anticipation of deep penetration, and I guided my cock through them, sheathing it in her warmth.

Melissa cried out from the intensity of my thrust as I went in too hard, but she knew better than to seek an escape. I pounded my way inside of her, breaking all of her defences until I could feel my orgasm building up. Not giving in to the temptation of slowing my pace, I pounded her with deep strokes until she was dripping with my hot spunk.

Only then did I let go, giving her a moment to catch her breath.

THE LIVING ROOM

I looked through the vertical blinds and feasted my eyes on the sunset. Powerful blasts of delicate orange filled the cloudy hints of the purple sky and at this moment, multiple random thoughts raced through my mind. I felt a presence beside me and turned sideways. My eyes stared deeply into the amorous eyes of my lover just before she looked away from me, and fixated her eyes on the sunset.

"Nice view, huh?" She rested her head on my shoulder and wrapped an arm around me.

"Not as nice as your sexy body though," I said.

I knew my word would fetch me her undivided attention. She looked up into my eyes the same moment I stared down at her. I planted a kiss on her forehead and squeezed her ass through her pants.

Fully facing her, I heaved her off the floor and positioned her on the sofa where I lay her down with a sinister smile. My hands slid up her legs and I parted her thighs to reveal her already wet pussy. She bit her lower lip as she watched me bow down to her juicy pussy.

With a soft moan, she relaxed her body, welcoming me into her temple. I started with a gentle kiss on her clitoral hood. I went around in circles, occasionally kissing her inner thighs. I moved in towards her labia, biting softly as I pulled her skin apart with my teeth. Feeling her juices on my lips, I parted her graciously and started to flick my tongue around her pussy. I pushed back the hood of her clit with a firm pressure to elicit a moan.

She sat up, pushed me back on the sofa in an attempt to dominate me. Once she got me to lay on my back, she mounted my face and settled her pussy on my mouth. I gulped heavily, swallowing every drop of nectar that made it to my tongue. Keeping her legs firmly positioned on both sides of my head, she dived forward and crowned my cock with her warm moist lips.

KINKY CRAVINGS

ABOUT THE AUTHOR

Jamal Walker

I guess you already know a lot about me after reading such a book. For those of you who are wondering. No, I do not have the luck to carry out all of these scenes as my wife is not into these kinks. However, I chose to write about them and share them with the world in hope that some of you may carry them out for me. Who knows maybe one day she'll open up to me and tell me her kinks too.

On the other hand, I am just another human trying to enjoy life in 2021, trying to get through this corona pandemic. They keep saying they are going to lift the lockdown, but who knows. I hope this book gives everyone something to entertain them whilst we wait to be allowed out again.
I enjoy cars, women and unsurprisingly forex because who doesn't do forex in this day and age.